Aunt Eater's Mystery
Halloween

story and pictures by
Doug Cushman

SCHOLASTIC INC.
New York Toronto London Auckland Sydney
Mexico City New Delhi Hong Kong

ISBN 0-439-22884-0

12 11 10 9 8 7 6 5 4 3   1 2 3 4 5/0

Printed in the U.S.A.   23

First Scholastic printing, September 2000

Contents

Aunt Eater Sees a Monster

Aunt Eater the anteater

put on her Halloween costume.

"It's perfect!" she said.

"I look like a real detective.

Now I must hurry.

I do not want to be late

for the big party

at Mr. and Mrs. Troop's house.

Everyone will be there."

She walked out the door,

turned the corner, and saw . . .

. . . a pirate!

"Oh my!" she said.

"Is that you, Wally?"

6

"I need help!" said Wally.

"There is a monster in my kitchen!

It has eaten my father!"

"That is silly," said Aunt Eater.

"There are no such things

as monsters."

"Come with me and see," said Wally.

Aunt Eater followed Wally

to the back door of his house.

"Look in there," whispered Wally.

Aunt Eater peeked around the door.

She saw a shadow on the wall.

"It does *look* like a monster,"

said Aunt Eater.

"OOOHHH!" it cried.

"It does *sound* like a monster,"

said Aunt Eater.

She closed the door again.

"My father and I just got home

from trick-or-treating," said Wally.

"My father went into the kitchen.

Then I heard scary noises.

Now he has not come back!"

"I do not believe in monsters,"

said Aunt Eater.

"I am going inside."

"Be careful!" cried Wally.

"The monster will eat you!"

"OOOHHH!" cried the monster.

Aunt Eater slowly opened the door.

She spied a trail of candy wrappers.

It went behind the table

to where the monster howled.

There was Wally's father.

"OOOHHH!" he moaned.

"I ate too much candy.

I feel sick."

16

"This mystery is solved,"

said Aunt Eater.

"I think this monster needs

a cup of tea

and a good night's sleep."

Aunt Eater Sees a Ghost

Aunt Eater walked past

Mr. Chumly's house.

Just then the door opened.

Out stepped a turnip!

"What a funny costume,"

said Aunt Eater.

"I am dressed as my favorite food,"

said Mr. Chumly.

"Are you going to the Troops' party?"

"Of course," said Aunt Eater.

"Let's walk together."

Aunt Eater and Mr. Chumly

walked down the dark street.

They passed a big, hollow tree.

"There is the Ghost Tree,"

said Mr. Chumly.

"People say a ghost

who has lost its head

lives inside."

"I do not believe in ghosts,"

said Aunt Eater.

21

Just then they heard,

"Help me! I'm lost!"

"What was that?" said Mr. Chumly.

Suddenly a pumpkin head

jumped out from the tree.

"Yikes!" cried Aunt Eater.

"It's the missing head!"

"Help me! I'm lost!" it cried again.

"Here I am, sweetie!"

said another voice.

They turned and saw

a ghost without a head!

It picked up the pumpkin head

and hugged it tight.

"I won't lose you again,"

said the ghost.

"Let's run away!"

cried Mr. Chumly.

"What is going on?"

said Aunt Eater.

"I've never heard of a ghost

calling its head 'sweetie'!"

"It is only me," said the ghost.

"Mrs. Crunch!" said Aunt Eater.

"You are not a ghost!"

"This is my costume.

I'm the ghost without a head,"

said Mrs. Crunch,

"but it is not a good costume.

It is too hard to see.

I lost my daughter Tilly."

"It is hard to see

out of my costume too,"

said Tilly.

"I couldn't find you."

"Let's go home," said Mrs. Crunch.

"We will find

some costumes that fit better

and will not scare our neighbors."

Aunt Eater laughed.

"I was so scared,

I almost lost *my* head!" she said.

Aunt Eater Hears Some Music

Aunt Eater and Mr. Chumly

arrived at the party.

A band was playing dance music.

Everyone was dancing and talking.

"Welcome! Welcome!"

said Mr. and Mrs. Troop.

"Come inside and have a good time."

Aunt Eater heard "Achoo!"

She turned to see . . .

. . . a carrot with a snake!

"Hello, Miss Underbelly,"

said Aunt Eater.

"How is your pet snake today?"

"Karl has a cold,"

said Miss Underbelly.

"He is also hungry.

He keeps crawling away

to find some food.

I think I had better

get him something to eat."

The band stopped to rest.

Aunt Eater drank some punch

and ate a pumpkin cookie.

Suddenly someone cried, "Listen!"

Everyone stopped talking.

Music was coming from the piano.

But no one was there.

"There's a ghost in here!"

cried Mr. Troop.

The strange music played on.

No one would go near the piano.

Suddenly Miss Underbelly cried,

"Karl is missing!

I cannot find him!"

"Maybe the ghost got him,"

someone said.

"We must find him

before the ghost does!"

said Aunt Eater.

41

Everyone searched the house.

They looked under the table.

They looked in the punch bowl.

They even looked in the tuba.

But no one found Karl.

"Now we have two mysteries,"

said Aunt Eater.

The strange music went on.

"How do we make a ghost go away?"

asked Mrs. Troop.

Suddenly from the piano

they heard "Achoo!"

"Do ghosts sneeze?" asked Mr. Chumly.

Aunt Eater laughed.

"I think we have the answer

to both mysteries," she said.

Aunt Eater opened the top

of the piano.

There was Karl.

He slithered along the piano strings

and made the strange music.

"He was looking for something to eat,"

said Miss Underbelly.

"I guess he got stuck inside."

"That snake is a good piano player," said the band leader.

"I want to hire him for my band."

"How exciting," said Aunt Eater.

"What do you say to that, Karl?"

"Achoo!" said Karl.

Aunt Eater
Dances a Jig

Everyone was laughing and eating

at the Halloween party.

The band was playing

lively dance music.

A scarecrow tapped

Aunt Eater's shoulder.

"What a good costume,"

said Aunt Eater.

"Who are you?"

"I'm Mr. Fragg,"

said the scarecrow.

"May I have the next dance?"

"Yes," said Aunt Eater.

"Let me get something to drink.

Then we can dance."

Aunt Eater went to the punch bowl

and drank some punch.

A scarecrow tapped her shoulder.

"I am ready, Mr. Fragg," she said.

The music began.

Aunt Eater and the scarecrow

danced a jig.

Then they danced the jitterbug.

Finally, they danced a tango.

"That was fun,"

said Aunt Eater,

"but now I am very thirsty.

I need something to drink."

She walked back to the punch bowl.

"I'm sorry," said Mr. Fragg.

"I hurt my foot.

I cannot dance with you."

"What are you talking about?"

said Aunt Eater.

"We just danced a jig,

the jitterbug, and a tango!"

"But I have been sitting here

by the punch bowl,"

said Mr. Fragg.

"I cannot move my foot."

"Then who was my partner?"

said Aunt Eater.

Aunt Eater looked for the scarecrow.

She looked everywhere.

But she did not find him.

The party finally ended.

Aunt Eater walked home

with Mr. Chumly.

"Did you ever find out

who danced with you?" he asked.

"No," said Aunt Eater.

"Halloween is a very mysterious time.

Many strange things can happen.

I may never know

who my dance partner was,

but he was a great dancer!"